I0537505

RISKY LOVE

Book 1

"*Alexandra's* LOVE & ROMANCE"™ *Series*

By

Denise Daniella Darcy

Published by
Durango Publishing Corp.®

Published by: Durango Publishing Corp.®

Written by: Denise Daniella Darcy

www.DurangoPublishing.com

Email: books@DurangoPublishing.com

Acclaim for Denise Daniella Darcy and *RISKY LOVE*

"While Risky Love is #1 in the Alexandra Series, it really is a continuation of the Samantha's Love and Romance Series. Different characters, different plot, different ending, but the same contemporary romance that keeps you turning the pages wanting more.

"Love scenes are hot and heavy, the characters are real and believable, and the storyline moves along at a good pace. Good writing and I am now a DDD fan." – Susan Pontleroy

"I love Denise Daniella Darcy's books. One of the best parts that she does in all of her books is provide an alternate ending, which I really like. It keeps you guessing not only to the end, but past that to the second ending as well. A unique way of writing.

"I also like the length. Some readers prefer super long novels, but I like the ones that you can read without having to keep checking back because you can't remember some important detail. Getting lost in the complexities isn't for me. But keeping me interested and absorbed, that is what DDD does." – Julie Shelbry

"When looking for a romance story I often go to Kristan Higgins and Tracy Brogan. I recently came across Risky Love and am adding Denise Daniella Darcy to my favorite author list. She writes great contemporary romances, with believable but imperfect characters that are experiencing love in different situations. Sometimes a heart gets broken, and sometimes true love is found, but each story has real interaction between the characters. And I think a lot of people will see similarities between the story and their lives. Not necessarily hidden morals, but something to think about afterwards. At times it felt like DDD had been there listening in to my conversation with my friends. A unique talent to get the reader to feel like they are inside the lead characters head.

"Highly recommend this author and her love and romance series." – Nancy Andrews

"I really enjoyed this book. It was romantic and real and believable yet not over the top. Too often I find that the romance novels are too in depth and lose me somewhere along the way. Risky Love has a good story and interesting characters who could actually be your best friend, mother or

father. I like the shorter length also, where I can read it from start to finish and still keep track of everyone and what is happening.

"I am a fan and think that Denise Darcy has come up with a winning formula here." – Alexis Hargraves

"The start of another successful series. One of the things I like best is that while the stories are short overall, I find that each one has kept me interested and entertained. I know that I am going to follow the rest in this series. I have read the Samantha series and loved the character development and interaction between them. Realistic. I found myself secretly cheering for Alex as she encountered problems with her best friend, something that I think most people can directly relate to.

"The story was presented well, good attention to detail and had a really good romance with a twist. Look forward to #2." – Bianca Tipton

"Risky Love has it all; steamy romance, great characters, and a couple of creative and interesting endings. Kept me entertained from start to finish. " – W. Good

Also by Denise Daniella Darcy

Samantha's

LOVE & ROMANCE Series

First Love – Book 1

Rebound Love Book 2

Cowboy Love – Book 3

Casual Love – Book 4

Also by Denise Daniella Darcy

Alexandra's

LOVE & ROMANCE Series

Risky Love – Book 1

Candid Love Book 2

Comic Con Love – Book 3

Special Love – Book 4

FREE BONUS – ALTERNATE ENDINGS

Hi Readers, Denise here. I just wanted to let you know that I have an unexpected bonus for you. I have written an alternate ending for RISKY LOVE, and it is yours absolutely free.

Why, you may ask? Simple. I always strive to give more than the anticipated, more than the normal. The alternate ending dramatically changes the outcome and is interesting, unique and original.

Click on this link to access your FREE alternate ending:

http://www.denisedanielladarcy.com/riskylovealtending

Just my way of giving you something extra and thanking you for reading my books.

I am busy writing more stories in my Love and Romance series so check my website at http://www.DeniseDaniellaDarcy.com for the most up-to-date list. Or just get my FREE newsletter to stay on top of new developments. Available at: www.denisedanielladarcy.com/newsletter.

Happy reading -

Denise Daniella Darcy

PS. And as an added SPECIAL BONUS, at the end of this story I have attached a SNEAK PREVIEW of CANDID LOVE, Book 2 in the series. Enjoy!

FYI - The stories in Alexandra's LOVE & ROMANCE Series can be read in any order. The stories are linked but each one is a separate story. Research has shown that most readers do prefer to read them in sequence.

Other Titles By Durango Publishing Corp.®

YOUR 'Lose Weight FAST the Natural & Healthy-Way DIET', a simple healthy weight loss diet so YOU can live a better, happier, more enjoyable life!

Horse Racing: Gambling to Win

Vegas Pro´s Best Racing Angles

Available at:

www.DurangoPublishing.com

www.DeniseDaniellaDarcy.com

&

Amazon

Table of Contents

Chapter 1 -- Fat ass and twig

"Oh yes baby, that's it! Work it for me darling! There you go!" The heavy sound of seductive words flowed over the dull throbbing beat of generic techno trash music with a practiced familiarity, like an experienced cowboy breaking in a new steed. *"Come on darling, show daddy what you've got?"*

A soft giggle elicited in exchange for the flirty conversation, soft, plump lips closing suggestively over one French tipped finger. *"Oh there we go love, that's it!"* The exchange was one sided, heavily sensuous and laden with delicious promise, words of whispered sensuality exchanged for the heated flush on pale cheeks. The bold, hungry anticipation of a deeper, more intimate conversation hidden just below the surface of the words flush with innuendo.

Alex looked on amazed, mesmerized and more than a little embarrassed as her best friend posed and modeled with such brazen sexuality. Gabriel and Alex had met in school way back when boys still had cooties and all discussions revolved around why Fluttershy was a much cuter pony than Applejack.

Their friendship had begun, as many lifelong bonds do, in the mutual admiration of tiny animals at the local pet shop and the semi-fanatical obsession that most little girls have with all things pink and fluffy and Barbie. Their shared interests had ended with their passage into womanhood, their paths sometimes taking diametrically opposite turns.

Gabby discovered boys, Alex discovered cameras. Gabby dated the quarterback, Alex fell in love with Andrew Prokos and Robert Mapplethorpe and James Nachtwey. Gabby lost a father to divorce,

Risky Love

Alex lost a mother to a drunken driver. There were very few things that were common to both their lives, in terms of their tastes, lifestyles, and who they were, but there was one thing which remained constant in their lives no matter what highs and lows they faced: each other.

Gabby was always there for Alex, and Alex was always there for Gabby, without question, without fail, without conditions. It did not matter what the occasion was, or how silly the other one felt, if it was important to one of them it was important to both of them. Which is why there were several dozen expired Comic Con passes in the back of Gabby's closet at home and an equal number of free gift bag skeletons in Alex's room.

It was also why Alex was here today. Gabby was modeling for one of the most prestigious talent companies in the country. Alex was here for moral support, or as

Gabby liked to call it, "free food and shirtless dudes".

The shoot finally over, Gabby strutted over to the side where Alex had managed to hide herself in the dim shadows, away from the glare of the strobe lights and camera flashes. Unlike Gabby, Alex found her peace behind the lens rather than in front of it.

"Hey beyotch!" Gabby exclaimed with a volume that made the spot boys look up in her direction.

Alex laughed and embraced her fondly, smiling at her as she spoke, "You look like a tramp!"

Gabby giggled and batted her eyes with a mock display of happiness. "Really?" she gushed. "You mean that?"

Alex nodded reassuringly. "A trampy tramp McTrampenstein from the town of Trampville," she reassured Gabby, who just shook her head and hugged Alex again, this time a much tighter embrace.

"I missed you, you crazy person." The words were spoken with a tone of sincerity that Gabby reserved for very few people. Alex smiled and squeezed her arms tight against Gabby wordlessly, her sincerity was expressed in far more silent expressions.

"Come on," Alex murmured, gently rubbing her friend's arm. "Let's get out of here, I can feel my IQ dropping just being in here."

Gabby smiled and shook her head. "Any lower and it is going to be in single digits," she remarked with a sly grin on her lips as she slipped her purse onto her arm and sauntered with her other arm locked with Alex's, spot boys gawking after her with a desperate pining that Gabby was all too used to.

She was a stunning thing; at five foot eight she was all legs and lips and cheekbones and sultry gaze. Both of them had the same exotic olive skin tone thanks to their Italian and Hispanic heritage and a childhood spent making mudpies under the sun, long dark hair and big brown eyes, both of which they shared like sisters born to the same mother.

Their bond was further strengthened by the intertwined network of family, friends, and neighbors, and the complex tangle of the pseudo-relationships of acquaintances, friends of friends and that-guy-who-is-friends-with-that-guy-ships, all of which had woven the two friends closer, far more than any blood relation could.

The pair walked out into the parking lot, Gabby leaving a trail of broken hearts in her wake and Alex barely looking up from the display of her trusty Canon SLR, the one that she always kept with her. She only looked up once she heard the roar of Gabby's car, brought around for her by another love struck valet. The look on the poor guy's face caused Alex to burst out chuckling.

Gabby was her best friend, her closest confidante, but that fact did not blind her from the girl's shortcomings. Gabby always had to be the center of attention. She thrived the most whenever she was in the limelight. This need was one of the only truly ugly things about her.

None of her other faults ever led Gabby into behavior as destructive as this need to be validated by the attention of others and it was something that Alex worried greatly about. Just as much as Gabby worried about Alex's opposite reaction to attention of any kind.

Alex smiled softly at her friend as she slid herself into the driver's side of the car, the two friends sharing over a decade's worth of laughter and heartbreak, tears and secrets, pinky promises and stubborn sulking silences

"Get in fat ass!" Gabby interrupted Alex's musings with a cheerfully brazen insult, one that caused Alex to only laugh and reply equally cheerfully, "Says the twig", the sound of the pair's laughter mingled with the roar of the high end roadster as it sped away out of the studio parking lot.

Chapter 2 -- The bond of cameras

The rest of the afternoon was spent in that warm, familiar, comfortable cocoon that comes with the closeness of best friends and may only be experienced by two girls spending a fully stocked credit card with no regard to the consequences of the bills to be paid.

The fully stocked credit card courtesy of Gabby's latest 'boyfriend', the term used in the very loosest sense of the word, as what Gabby called their relationship was defined by the most basic satisfaction of his need to have a 20 something model on his arm and her need to have fully stocked credit cards in her purse.

It was an arrangement that Alex would have balked at but one that Gabby brazenly, happily embraced without the slightest hesitation. As far as she was concerned it was HIS money and HIS choice to spend it however he wished. It was yet another area where the two friends agreed to respectfully disagree.

Ostensibly the shopping trip was to prepare for the birthday party of Alex's dad. But in between shopping for the perfect smoking pipe and fishing rod, which young girl could ever deny the temptation of a caramel frappe from the nearest Starbucks or that deliciously overpriced pair of boots that are so utterly impractical but oh-so-necessary to have.

By the end of the trip their luggage consisted of two bags of party supplies and presents, and five of personal items, all of which were dumped gleefully, unashamedly into the back seat of Gabby's car, to be explained at a later time.

The Luciano residence was an ancestral four story house that had been built originally as a ranch and farm. The inevitable years of modernization and industrialization had rendered the original intentions obsolete but it still sported the vast land necessary for exercising horses and rearing livestock.

It was the perfect place for a child to grow up in, with plenty of room to run and scream and chase after imaginary friends, lots of perfect hidden corners to conceal secrets in and plot out childish schemes.

For most of her friends a trip to Alex's house was a treat, made even more enjoyable by the warmth that her late mother exuded. Their house had always been open for sleepovers and birthday parties and barbecues, and broken windows and vases were quickly swept under the rug. The guilt of such destruction assuaged by a batch of warm, homemade, oven-fresh cookies and a kindly smile.

Even after the untimely passing of Alex's mom the tradition was continued by her father, a gruff and exuberant man not given to subtleties and silence. He managed to keep his family life together, sacrificing a promising career as a combat journalist whom Time magazine had in one article described as 'part pit bull part Picasso'.

Yet he left it all behind to care for his orphaned daughter, to rebuild the shattered wreckage of his family. His exploits frozen in 10" x 10" photo frames, showing the various pieces of his former life, now decorated the wall of his study and private offices. He had not had to duck under the sound of bombs going off for more than a decade and yet he was still best known for his intrepid coverage during the Balkan wars and a dozen other conflicts around the planet.

None of them had forgotten the pit bull, least of all his daughter. He had been the primary inspiration that led her to get behind the lens of a camera for the first time. The first camera she had ever received was a cheerily bright Canon with a uselessly fragile plastic frame, that was a gift he had mailed to her on her 11th birthday from his assignment in Kosovo. One of many cheap knockoffs that were being sold like … well … cheap knockoffs in the streets of the European city.

It had been more than just a hobby for young Alexandra, it was a method of getting closer to her father. There is little commonality between the interests of daughters and fathers as it is, and Lawrence Luciano was further alienated from his offspring by the eccentricities and requirements of his job.

The camera was the link that bound them together, their correspondence consisted of her asking his advice as to the best angles to shoot her teddy bears at, how best to capture the delicate nuances of photographing the neighbors litter of recently born puppies and various other subtleties of the craft that bound father and daughter.

They had had to force themselves to find fresh avenues for bonding a year later after they lost the one great mooring of their lives. And they had. Lawrence had learned to appreciate the dynamics of female teenager social life and Alex gained a deeper respect and insight of jazz music and second hand cigar smoke.

Alex had been extremely lucky in the adaptability and versatility of her father, who had been forced to mold himself into a variety of roles. Father, mother, best friend, confidante, protector, teacher, provider, official worrier, all the different hats that a pair of parents would share among themselves, Lawrence had been forced to juggle all together at the same time.

Their extended family helped greatly, there was nary a weekend when some Auntie or Uncle was not visiting, there was no shortage of Grandmas and Grandpas to pamper and coddle and spoil and treat Alex, but in the end it was always Alex and her father, and they had done quite well for themselves.

They would always feel the pain of their loss but they had dealt with it together, and Alex had been nothing but happy for her father when he had announced that he would be inviting Cynthia to his birthday party, Alex had been looking forward to meeting her father's girlfriend for quite some time now.

Chapter 3 -- Princess puppy eyes

"HAPPY BIRTHDAY!" The room erupted in a cheerful, raucous chorus as soon as Lawrence opened the door. The inside of his home had been decorated with silver and black balloons, green buntings hung from every available edge and corner, a spider web of papery decorations that hung low over the heads of the guests with pointy paper hats on their heads.

The greeting was met with a surprised gasp from Lawrence as he walked into his own home, surprised even though he had full knowledge of what his daughter had been planning for him. Part of being a father to Alex was to pretend half the time to not knowing what was going on and being an all knowing demi-god the other half of the time.

For today though, all he had to be was a spoiled and loved father. "What is this?" He laughed softly as he embraced his daughter.

"Happy Birthday pop," Alex grinned happily as she squeezed her arms around her father.

"Did you know about this?" Lawrence asked Cynthia, turning back towards her. The two had walked in holding hands and they hadn't parted them yet.

Seeing that comforted Alexandra greatly. Her father had devoted himself to her upbringing with a fierce single-minded purpose that bordered on the fanatical. For the past ten years she had not seen him go out on a single date. What she had seen were the appearance of several grey hairs in that lush, rich, dark mane of his. All of them caused by staying up late waiting for her to get home, or worrying about what major she is going to take in college, or the lack of any boyfriends ever since the last breakup in her senior year of high school.

The pressures of two parents brought to bear down on his broad shoulders. And shoulder those responsibilities he had, admirably. Alex just wanted him to settle down now, not an easy proposition on the other side of 50, but she was hopeful nevertheless and incredibly grateful for the entry of Cynthia into their lives, into his life in particular.

The pair had met at one of Lawrence's client's gallery openings. His studio routinely did work for fashion houses and artists and would customarily be invited to the events marking the culmination of their work. Cynthia worked as a public relations expert for one of such firms.

Gabby liked to claim credit for introducing the two, seeing as how it was the fashion house she was modeling for at the time which employed Cynthia, but Alex believed it was deeper. Her father had a saying that there is a time for everything and when the time for a particular thing has come, there was no way it could be avoided.

Simply put, it was time for Lawrence to find love again, and even though she had been overseas on a Nat Geo internship assignment and had only met Cynthia via webcam, she had a really good feeling about the woman.

"I had absolutely no clue," Cynthia said with a soft chuckle.

Her blue eyes twinkling warmly, there was an air of old school elegance about her, something that reminded people of an era when femininity was strength and grace, and not just sex appeal. Alex smiled happily at the look that passed between her father and Cynthia.

"If I had told you, you would have simply ditched us all," Alex said with laughter in her voice.

Lawrence was not someone who was particularly fond of crowds, preferring a smaller, tighter circle of friends and family, fishing trips and jazz music to large gatherings of semi strangers and vague acquaintances. Lawrence shrugged lazily, "I woulda shown up for the cake," he quipped, with that trademark languid wit of his before pecking a soft kiss on his daughter's cheek.

"Now," he said with a smile, "I would like you to meet someone." The boyish twinkle in his gaze made Alex's heart melt and the smile she had on her lips could not have been more genuine as her father introduced Cynthia. "This is Cynthia," he said with a soft charmed tone to his voice that she had not heard in ten years.

"Hello Cynthia," she said before embracing her in a surprised hug, one that Cynthia returned after a moment of hesitation. "Welcome." The word was spoken with sincerity and gladness that she felt deeply towards the woman who had made her father smile after so long.

The party lasted until well after midnight, egged on by drunken stories of Lawrence's youth and of his incredulous bravery. His tales of rash bravery and dedication to his craft seemed like some pleasant fiction to Alex. To her he was always the level headed, practical parent, the one who always fretted about her not having a stable job or not having a boyfriend, or not getting enough to eat, or not calling him enough.

She could never imagine him as the brash hot-headed combat photographer who had allegedly gotten into a Hutu warlord's face with his camera, clicking away photographs of him even when the warlord had poked the barrel of his AK-47 at his head. Such tales seemed complete fabrications to her and she simply smiled and nodded along to them until the guests dribbled away one by one and only the family was sitting around the table, Alex and Gabby, Cynthia and Lawrence.

"So," Lawrence began with a sigh of contentment, nursing a scotch in one hand, "How would you feel about giving your old man a hand?"

Alex had heard this pitch before, her father attempting to reel her into working for him under the guise of 'giving her old man a hand'. "Dad … come on …" she said with a well-meaning frustrated smile on her lips.

"No, seriously," he interrupted. "I am not kidding, we really need a couple of extra hands around the studio." He fished inside his pockets and pulled out a card for a 'Le bel inconnu'.

Alex had no sooner taken the card before Gabby squealed excitedly, "ohmygod ohmygod ohmygod ohmygod!" She clutched at the card, tugging it from Alex's hands.

"Can I come too? Please Mr.Luciano? Please? Please? Please?" She grasped at Lawrence's wrist with both hands tugging on it insistently, prompting a puzzled look from Alex.

"What the hell?" she muttered under her breath. "What exactly is going on here?" She glanced from Gabby to her father and back again, and Gabby snorted in derision, "Oh like YOU would know." She rolled her eyes at Alex as if she had just asked her who Bono is.

Lawrence smiled politely at Gabby and patted her wrist. "Of course you can come darling," and added quickly before Gabby could explode with sheer glee, "If Alex allows it."

Immediately Gabby's expression changed from haughty ice princess to princess puppy eyes and all Alex could do was laugh and shake her head before shrugging. "Sure," she spoke with a playful twinkle in her eyes, "I could use an assistant."

Lawrence and Alex shared a knowing smile. Alex knew she had been played into taking this assignment and by God she was going to pay him back in kind.

Chapter 4 -- Green eyes

"I am SO gonna get back at him," Alex muttered under her breath as she stood at the front door of her father's studio, the inside of which was populated entirely by concentrated groupings of utterly gorgeous male models, most of whom looked like they had just walked off a J.Lo music video.

Apparently 'Le bel inconnu' was a highly regarded male modeling service, which would explain why Gabby had been oh so very excited about Alex being asked to work on this project. It also explained why Lawrence had been so adamant on getting Alex on this shoot. Not only would it put money in Alex's pocket but she would also have the chance to land a date.

'Hah!' Alex thought to herself with a self-assured smug. 'That's what HE thinks! I'll show him … I am not going to date anyone at all! That'll teach him,' she groaned inwardly at her self-destructive defiance. Do as father asks and get some digits from hot, six- pack sporting bona fide models? Or put your foot down and end up a crazy cat lady at 65?

She had to admit, she had been played very well by her father. At the very least she would get to spend some time with Gabby. "Gabby?" she called out as she looked around for her friend who moments ago had been by her side but had somehow magically managed to transport herself into the middle of a circle of five eagerly grinning male models, apparently appraising their chiseled torsos to decide which one would be first. For the photo-shoot, obviously.

Alex grinned softly, she had to hand it to the girl. She did NOT waste any time at all. Alex shook her head with a soft, exasperated sigh as she walked over to her work station and dumped her bag on the table provided for her. Nimble fingers worked deftly to attach different lenses, trying each one for focus and clarity and a dozen other variables familiar only to professionals or dedicated enthusiasts.

She would have to work alone for the time being as her 'assistant' was otherwise engaged, mainly in the pursuit of being worshiped by hunky models. The preparation procedure was more than just standard technique, it had a calming influence on Alex, allowed her to center her mind, to put aside her anxieties and eccentricities, to slip comfortably into the skin of someone who knew what she was doing, who loved her craft and practiced it with skilled grace.

"HEADS UP!!" Alex spun around at the loud shout to watch one of the tallest men in the group come charging towards her, his head looking back over his shoulder, eyes on the ball that someone had brought to the studio and had apparently thought would be a good idea to toss around.

Alex reacted with all the present mindedness and agility of a park pigeon. She froze in place. 'This is it,' thought Alex 'This is how I die.' She closed her eyes shut tightly and scrunched her body up as compactly as she could, all highly effective measures when about to be run over by a six foot five, twenty something guy. 'Death by male model, how ignominious' were the last thoughts through her head as she braced for impact and what she was sure would be a very painful collision.

Luckily for Alex the impact never came. What came instead was the sound of a pair of bodies crashing onto the table behind her, a woosh of air as the body tumbling towards her was tackled and pushed out of its trajectory. Alex peeked out of one eye to look around her feet at the crushed remnants of the table she had just laid out her equipment on and the tangled bodies of two of the models.

Apparently a quick thinking individual had managed to tackle the slower thinking one away from her and in the process crashed onto the table. "Oh no!" Alex gasped as she kneeled down immediately besides the awkward crash pile of the two men. Her attentions were instead focused on the pile of her own equipment now scattered around the debris of the table. "Oh you fucking IDIOTS!"

She shrieked the words out before she could hear them in her head. Her fingers trembled as she sifted anxiously through her bag checking for damage to her precious camera, her lenses and other delicate equipment, each one of which she loved and cherished, not to mention depended on for her livelihood.

She turned her head angrily towards the tangle of bodies that were responsible for the crash and found herself staring into the most seductively mystifying pair of green eyes that she had ever seen in her life. "Oh we aren't all that bad." She heard the voice that went along with the eyes and it made her entire body tingle and all of a sudden all her anger drained from her body leaving only the reddish flush on her cheeks.

She stood up flustered and the stranger who had saved her stood up with her, a smile on his face. "Look, I'm really sorry about all this," he said with a boyish grin on his lips that dimpled his cheeks in the most adorable way. "How about I take you out for dinner after the shoot to make it up to you?" The way he said it, in the most innocuous matter of fact way, with that easy confidence.

Alex couldn't do anything but giggle like a thirteen year old schoolgirl. She quickly cleared her throat and forced the happy expression off her face and despite her best efforts all she could do was murmur a soft, "Sure, why not." And with that example of the seductive wiles of Alex Luciano she excused herself hastily to move towards the 'Work area' designated exclusively for photography and modeling.

Her assignments were usually the high point of her day but today it felt like they were a mere distraction and each time she focused her camera lens on another model, all she could see was those gorgeous green eyes staring back up at her. When finally the lunch break came she put her camera down, waited for a full five minutes at the work station before she made her way towards the waiting room where the models yet to be photographed, green eyes among them, were waiting.

Alex paused at the door and took a deep breath, took a moment to look into her reflection in the back of her phone and repeated her personal mantra, "Don't be weird," before she pushed open the door and walked in on Green Eyes and Gabby making out passionately.

Chapter 5 -- Cold-shoulder bug

"Oh wow," Gabby gasped huskily as she rolled onto her back in the bed she had shared last night with Adam 'Green eyes' Thompson. The sheets clung to her body drenched with sweat, her dark hair spilled messily onto the pillow underneath her head as she turned to look at Adam who was in the same stage of sweaty, barely breathing sated contentment.

"That was amazing," she gushed with a soft giggle in her voice as she leaned up to kiss at his chiseled jaw before falling back with a happy sound against the bed, the sheets now carelessly slipped low on her body, exposing her pert breasts.

Adam and Gabby had been dating now for the better part of three weeks. They had hit it off ever since their first meeting at Alex's photo studio and it had been lust at first sight. Adam was a prime specimen of male virility and attractiveness, or as Gabby had so succinctly put it five minutes after watching him strip down into a tight red sports speedo: 'Ay Papi!'

At six feet one, he easily towered over the statuesque and runway ready Gabby, a physique chiseled to perfection over a life time of physicality that began in his early childhood when mother Thompson first introduced baby green eyes to the wonderful world of Karate.

It gave his body the lean, solid yet supple framework that would be later enhanced by the growing solid mass of corded muscle, honed to rippling perfection in the gym and embellished by hours upon hours of playing shirtless soccer in the sun. His mixed heritage of Irish and Greek parents afforded him that gorgeous tinge of exoticism that stirred fire in the bellies of most girls, the Greek side of his family responsible for those seductive green eyes and those dimples a gift of the Irish.

He was the perfect mix of the erotic and the adorable, that delicate balance between mysteriously, sexually charged masculinity that made Gabby's knees go weak and that playful, charming boyishness that made her heart skip joyously.

She didn't want to admit it but she perhaps enjoyed his company a bit more than her usual amorous interactions with muscled hunks. Although what little time they spent together was hardly ever wasted on the mundane stuff like conversations and dates and shared meals, instead they focused on what was truly important: the mutual exploration of lustful desires and fiery passions, the submerging of their souls and beings into a hedonistic explosion of each other's body.

In the three weeks they had been 'seeing' each other, both of them would agree that they did not spend more than a cumulative 24 hours of time with their clothes on. It was an arrangement that both of them seemed perfectly at ease with.

Today however, Gabby had other things on her mind apart from spending long, sweaty, heated hours between the sheets with Adam, and he sensed it without her needing to say a word. "Something on your mind?" he asked as he rolled onto his side to better look at Gabby. A curious smile on his face, one arm reached to drape across her bare chest, his hand cupping lazily against her dark nipple and gently fondling it, an act of fondness and affection.

Gabby smiled up at him, rolling to her left to face him, one hand moving over his muscled chest, tracing the perfectly symmetrical lines carved out by countless pushups and bench presses. "It's Alex," she spoke after a few greedy moments of fondling him. "I'm kind of worried about her."

Things had been extremely awkward on that first day when Alex had walked in on her and Adam making out in the waiting room. Gabby had no idea what had happened and the only thing she knew for certain was that her one true best friend in her life was building walls around her.

In the last few weeks Alex had claimed one assignment after another, keeping Gabby at an arm's distance and had even minimized communication with her to a bare minimum. She had no idea what was going on with her and no amount of cajoling, arguing, or manipulating would get the truth out of her. It was as if Alex had suddenly been bitten by the 'cold-shoulder' bug.

Gabby sighed and snuggled her face against Adam's neck, her slender manicured fingers once again lazily fondling over his chiseled torso, this time admiring the firmness of his half a dozen abdominal muscles. He calmed her somewhat, made her feel like a normal girl, something she had not felt like since she had been fourteen and signed her first modeling contract with a teen magazine.

Since then her life had taken on a touch of the surreal and everything in it had been fashioned and molded and repurposed to suit her career and her ambitions. Adam was the one thing that did not fit into any of those categories. He was not connected to the industry other than being part of it the same as she was. He was not some rich trust fund kid whom she could milk for gifts and favors. In fact nothing about him made practical sense for her to be with, which is why Gabby felt so utterly drawn to him. He was beginning to feel more and more like an island of calm in an ocean of crazy to her.

Chapter 6 -- Memories of mom

Alex sat in her mother's room by the window, an old picture of her father and mother held in her hands. It was an old one, taken in the late seventies, the color slightly faded from the photograph but not from her mother's eyes in the picture.

She traced against the contour of her parents in the picture, her fingertip leaving a smudged line in the thin film of dust on the glossy surface. Had her dad really sported bell bottoms? What in the world was her mother thinking with that hairstyle? They looked like complete strangers in that captured moment. In fact, if no one told her that she was looking at her parents, she would not have guessed it in a hundred years.

Her earliest memories of her mother involved sensible mom jeans and soft plaid shirts that always smelled of cinnamon and sage and thyme and a magical combination of herbs and spices and crayon dust. Alex always missed her. Her memory was like the dull throbbing ache of an old wound that never really goes away and flares up sharply, painfully on wet, rainy days.

Today was one of those days. She did not even realize that she was crying until she saw her tears drop down onto the dusty glass frame of the photograph she was holding. Her eyes shut tightly, bravely against the salty sting of tears behind her eyes as she hugged the photograph against her chest and lowered her head against her knees.

"Alex? Darling?" The soft voice at the door made her sit up abruptly.

"Just a minute!" Her voice came out far more bleary and watery than she would have liked and she hurried to wipe at her tears as she opened the door. "Oh ... hey Cynthia." Alex tried to keep the trembling out of her voice and even managed a brave smile. "I didn't know you were here," Alex mumbled distractedly as she moved away from the door towards the stacked boxes, her mother's legacy neatly packed away.

"Actually," Cynthia began as she closed the door behind her, "Lawrence called me over, he wanted me to talk to you."

Alex turned to look at her, a smile flickering on her lips. So much in her life was because of her father, because of his constant, sometimes frustrating concern for his daughter. "You didn't have to," Alex said with a genuine smile on her lips. "He just worries too much."

Cynthia smiled in return, wordless and gentle, with that knowing look in her eyes that only a mother may know. "You know, I don't think I told you this before but I knew your mother."

Alex arched a brow at Cynthia's words. "Really?" she said. "When? How?"

Cynthia shrugged and casually picked up a cookbook, one of many packed into a carton. "We were actually in the same sorority back in college," Cynthia said, her eyes filled with misty nostalgia. "Before she met your dad, she actually initiated me into the sorority."

Alex settled down on an old creaky settee. "I didn't know that," Alex said with a growing fascination for this woman. "Dad never said anything."

Cynthia shrugged casually as she spoke. "You know those people you meet sometimes who are everything you ever want to be? People who have every single quality that you hoped you could have, do the things that you wish you could do, say the things you wished you could say?"

Alex nodded silently, she knew that feeling all too well for far too long.

"Your mother was that person for me." Alex smiled softly at the older woman's admission. She hadn't known Cynthia for more than a week and here she was baring her soul.

"I wish I could say that we were good friends," Cynthia continued, "But the fact of the matter was that we were little more than acquaintances. Sure we knew each other and said hello to each other and smiled and waved, but I really doubt if she even remembered my name." Alex nodded as Cynthia spoke. "But that's the thing, I don't remember her speaking to me on more than a few occasions but even with this limited amount of interaction I knew instinctively what kind of a woman she was." Cynthia sighed and walked over to where Alex was sitting and sat down beside her. "And I know how much she would hate for you to be feeling whatever you are feeling right now."

Alex bit her lip at Cynthia's words and immediately felt her throat knot up. Absurdly, she felt guilty for feeling the way she did. Gabby was her best friend and Adam was some guy she barely met, she had no right to resent the two their happiness. But something deep inside her, something beyond logic and reason was outraged, was angry and deeply sorrowful. Whatever she had felt with Adam, whatever that moment was that they shared, she knew it was worth more than it seemed, in that moment she knew exactly what her father always used to talk about when he used to discuss stories of meeting Alex's mother.

It just wasn't fair. "It's not fair," Alex whispered, the words heavily weighed by the stress of the grief they carried. She shook her head and pulled her knees up against her chest, resting her head on top of them. "Why not me?" Alex whimpered softly, her lashes closing over wet cheekbones. "It isn't fair," Alex repeated and Cynthia wrapped her arms around Alex's trembling frame and held her as tightly as she could, trying, or at least attempting to replicate some of the strength and warmth that Alex's mother would have wanted her to have.

Chapter 7 -- Short (short!) dress and an entourage

Alex fidgeted nervously as she stood in front of the mirror wearing the skimpy little Versace number she had been ordered into. Her heartfelt moment with Cynthia had led to another discovery by Alex of the older woman's personality, the one that doesn't take no for an answer.

Apparently one of Cynthia's exes, with whom she was on very good terms, was a major player in the club scene and was inaugurating a new establishment tonight. Alex was to visit this new club opening and have a good time.

Those were the details of her orders and despite her most vehement protests Alex had been powdered and pampered and glossed and curled and coiffed and utterly dolled up before being squeezed into a dress whose hem lay a full four inches above the line of the shortest dress she had ever worn.

The result was absolutely stunning. Alex was the same height as Gabby and shared the same rich, dark hair and gorgeous brown eyes as her, but where Gabby had trimmed her figure to a slender, graceful silhouette, Alex had the lush curves that filled out her clothes in a way that added a decadent sensuousness to her.

Cynthia walked in as Alex was tugging at the hem of the dress, trying to pull the fabric lower to keep it from its upward insistence. "Wow!" Cynthia exclaimed with a grin. "Good God woman! Don't you look like a heart-breaker!"

Alex smiled back at Cynthia, a shy blush on her cheeks as she shrugged and replied, "I'll be lucky if I don't turn into a neck-breaker by the end of the night," she giggled as she looked down at the six inch Loboutin stilettos she was standing in.

She was more of a Converse and Reebok kind of girl although Loboutin and D&G seemed like old, long lost friends on her. Cynthia smiled softly and walked up to Alex to squeeze her shoulders lightly. "Hey," Cynthia spoke in a gentle, familiar whisper, "Try and have fun tonight, alright? I know you really don't feel like it, but try anyway."

Alex looked up into her eyes before nodding, a smile on her lips. "Thanks Cyn, I will." Alex paused for a moment before she leaned forwards and wrapped her arms tightly around Cynthia. "Thank you," Alex spoke with genuine gratitude in her voice, she really was thankful to have Cynthia in her life at this moment.

Alex felt her hug returned warmly before Cynthia kissed her cheek. "Go have fun darling." Alex heard the same grateful tone in Cynthia's voice as well.

The opening was a noisy, clamorous affair with camera flashes and celebrity appearances galore, strictly red carpet and strictly A-list. Alex rubbed shoulders with more celebrities in the first ten minutes of arriving at the club than she had in her entire life at that moment and it took all her self-control not to go complete fan girl and start asking for autographs.

She was received right out of her car by the club coordinator (Alex had no idea there even existed such a job description) and led straight into the VIP section of the club, camera flashes lighting her way and every other paparazzi begging for a smile or a pose, a girl this smoking hot just HAD to be someone, didn't she?

Alex hadn't been so sure about this idea when Cynthia had first proposed it to her but now she was in complete agreement with her dad's girlfriend. This was a completely different world, surreal and glamorous, beautiful and deliciously superficial, full of pink martinis and trashy EDM music, impromptu photo shoots in dark corners of the VIP section and having the opportunity of grinding up on your celebrity crush since the eighth grade.

Cynthia had called ahead and arranged for things beforehand with her ex and wherever Alex went she was treated, literally, as royalty, and soon enough had gathered her own little entourage of ditzy, scantily clad climbers, friendly and loud and prone to getting the hunky bartenders that manned the four bars in the club to do shots off them. They were literally the complete opposite of what Alex looked for in her friends, but tonight she was immeasurably grateful for their company.

It meant Alex got to do shots off of bartender six-packs as well. It was at her second go around at feasting on smooth, hardened rippling abdominals when she heard a familiar voice. "Alex? Is that you?"

Alex turned around at the sound of her name to come face to face with Adam standing right behind her. "Oh!" That sound was the sound of three martinis and half a dozen tequila shots draining right out of her system. "Hi." That second sound was the sound of all her insecurities and fears and disappointments shooting right back into her system.

"What … uh … what are you doing here?" Alex stammered. "Where's Gabby?"

Adam smiled lightly down at her as he spoke, those damn eyes of his making her lips go dry. "I don't know … I'm here alone."

Alex arched a brow at those words and folded her arms across her chest. "You're here alone?"

There was a slight hard edge to her voice which made Adam laugh and raise his hands defensively. "Hey, I'm working!" He grinned and pointed to the club logo on his black T-shirt. "See?"

The sound of his laughter made her flush and she gripped at her arms tighter. "Sorry … I …" she began, unsure of what to say.

Adam interrupted her gently. "You what? You thought I was two timing Gabby?" Alex flushed deeper, shrugging wordlessly and looked away from him. "Alex," Adam said gently, "Gabby and I aren't an item, you know that right?"

Chapter 8 -- Slap and a kiss

"You and Gabby aren't a couple?" Alex repeated Adam's words monotonously, her expression blank.

Adam sighed and rubbed at the back of his neck. "Look ... I didn't mean for that to sound so bad," he grumbled under his breath. "I don't ..." he sighed as he tried to grope for words. "Look, I see what's going on between you and her, and I really don't want to be the cause of that."

Alex pursed her lips tightly at his words, her own spoken tersely, "and what makes you think you are the cause of anything?"

Adam blinked at the tone of her voice, his green eyes searching hers before he frowned slightly. "So, you're saying whatever this thing is between you and Gabby, I have no part in it?" He spoke with a growing annoyance, his arms folding across his chest as were Alex's.

"I'm saying it's none of your business whatever this 'thing' is between me and Gabby," Alex replied with a harsher sting to her words than she had intended.

Adam stared down at her, the back of his jaw clenched tightly. "You know," his words slipped through carefully measured restraint, "I am having a really hard time getting through to you, you haven't given me a single straight answer."

Alex bristled at his words, the soft, glossed line of her plush lips squeezed together tightly. "Well, maybe if you asked a straight question," Alex snapped back at him. "But so far all you have been doing is dancing around your words."

Adam's jaw clenched tighter and those green eyes flashed a bright glint and for a moment Alex felt her tummy clench. "How's this for straight then," Adam growled as he leaned forward and cupped the back of her neck, pressing his lips to hers in a firm, angry kiss.

Alex squealed her muffled surprise against his lips, her eyes snapping open in shock, her jaw slack as he pulled away from the kiss, that animal intensity burning in his eyes.

WHACK!

Alex had no idea where that came from, her slap against his cheek was more of a reflex action than a conscious response, the sound like a gun shot at the beginning of a race. For a moment they stared at each other in utter astonishment at what just happened, and then just as abruptly and violently as she had slapped him, she kissed him.

Her lips pressed to his with an angry, spirited hunger, one which he returned in kind as he squeezed her frame in his arms, his hard body crushing her curved figure in the most deliciously restrictive of ways. Alex felt her breath leave her lungs in a heated, moist gasp, her lips parting against the brash eagerness of Adam's mouth. Her own arms slid up over his back, caressing the sculpted contour of his back, she felt her knees tremble as one of his hands pressed against the small of her back while the other cupped the back of her head.

Alex's lips tingled with a pleasurable sting as he pulled his mouth off hers, his breath hot and panting against her skin. His hands moved over her body eagerly, brazenly, in a way that made her feel tiny and delicate and fragile. Alex looked up into his eyes and despite being in a tortuously loud and incredibly packed club, in that moment they were the only two people on the planet.

Chapter 9 -- Back room antics

"Why did you do that?" Adam whispered tenderly against her lips, nuzzling against her cheek.

Alex nuzzled back, brushing her cheek against his jaw. "Why did YOU do that?" Alex replied back and Adam just chuckled at her words.

"You are doing it again!" he whispered softly against her ear in a voice that made her close her eyes and shudder against his frame.

Alex leaned forward, pressing her forehead against the bulge of Adam's throat. "Gabby …" she whispered softly against the intoxicating scent of Adam's skin, unwilling to say more than that.

"Gabby," Adam continued for her, "and I are not an item." He gripped Alex's chin gently and tilted her head up towards him, meeting her gaze firmly. "We aren't together."

Alex sighed softly and caressed her fingers over that utterly, heart-breakingly gorgeous face of his. "Neither are we," she whispered softly against his lips, the urge to taste them again almost overwhelming.

"Aren't we?" Adam turned Alex to his right, pinning her against the bar counter, his smile rakish and hungry, the kind of look that the gods of seduction and one night stand-ery had designed solely to get girls to drop their panties.

Alex bit her lip, her slender manicured fingers gripping against the tight fabric of his shirt and before she could reply, his lips were crushed against hers, slower this time, indulgent and soft, a kiss like melting ice cream, moist and tender and utterly delicious.

This time when the kiss broke Adam was leading Alex towards the back of the

VIP section and Alex followed in a daze, her gloss slightly smudged against the corner of her mouth. The stride of her legs wobbled a little as Adam pulled her into another passionate embrace, tumbling the both them into the back room where beer crates and supply boxes were crammed floor to ceiling.

The door slammed shut behind Alex and she was pushed up against it. Her dark gaze met with Adam's and a moment of utter and complete animal understanding passed between them. Their smiles matched each other in the silent acknowledgment of their hunger and a moment later their bodies were a blur of stumbled, passionate embrace.

Alex moaned as she felt her panties being peeled off her. She tasted his essence between her teeth as she pressed them down a tad too hard against his throat. The throbbing, warm sensation of her passion leaked down against the inside of her thigh, encouraged by Adam's hungered exploration of her sex.

She whimpered a girlish exclamation as Adam turned her around and pinned her up against the door, his hand pressed against the middle of her shoulder blades holding her in position as he kneeled down behind her and yanked her dress up over her waist. She bit down on her fist as Adam growled behind her, his hot breath washing against her slick, eager sex, followed immediately by the sensation of his mouth on it. "Adam!" she stuttered out his name as his tongue went inside of her. She whimpered again as he bullied her clit, tugging on it, suckling on it, committing wet, passionate violence on it.

She rolled her head back, her long dark hair undone from its bun, and reached back with one hand, her fingers grasping at his hair and urging his hunger, mixing it with her own as she all but sat down on his face. The way he moved was a complete domination of her, his frame dwarfing hers, his strength guided by his hunger, his lust matching an animal's as he feasted on her. She had never felt so utterly small and fragile and vulnerable as he made her feel and it thrilled her at a very primal level like no one else had ever before.

"D-d-don't!" she whimpered, stuttering the word out before she clamped a hand over her mouth and screamed the celebration of her orgasm into it. It ripped through her like a tidal wave, drowning her, washing her away and flooding into her until she felt like she would burst. A soft whimper passed through her lips before she felt her legs give out. Adam moved forward, grasping her waist with one arm and helped her slip down onto his lap.

His breath caressed against her ear, soft kisses soothed her heated skin before Alex turned towards him, looking up at his face, her eyes a half-glazed screen of desire and lust as she crept her hands over his strong shoulders and helped him lean back and lay down on the cold, hard floor.

The warmth of her thighs straddling him a stark contrast against the cool of the tiles and the sound of his zipper being pulled down sounded louder than it should have. Alex leaned down and pressed her lips to his again, a gentle caress of his lips as her fingers tenderly curled around his throbbing hardness, squeezing curiously, eagerly. Her lips smothered the hungry groan that slipped past his lips, the kiss growing warmer, firmer as she pressed deeper and deeper into the kiss. Leaning forward she lifted her hips up and positioned herself over him before pressing herself down, sinking that thick shaft of his into her aching wetness.

Their groans intermingled in one single sound of ecstasy as she sank down on him, her eyes shut tightly as she reveled in the feeling of being so utterly and completely filled up. A sudden shiver ran up her spine as she felt Adam grasp her hips and move her down against him. She bit down on her bottom lip, her hands pressing down against his shoulders as she moved in the same rhythm of his hips grinding up against her, a slow sensuous dance with the both of them moving together as one, the sound of their heated breathing providing the music for their erotic duet.

Alex could feel the urgency of her desire coil tighter in the pit of her stomach, that delicious, moist stickiness that leaked down freely like nectar between her thighs as her body danced to the dictates of her lust. She leaned down once again, crushing Adam's mouth against hers and felt him shudder, his body responding like a twin to the shared pleasure of their exquisite mating. His voice a rasping growl, "I am going to cum." Alex moaned at that declaration and without thinking snapped her teeth against his bottom lip, cruelly tugging on the soft flesh of his mouth, pulling it upwards as far as it would go before letting it snap back against his mouth.

Her hips rode him with a frantic desperation, the sound of flesh clapping against flesh getting louder and louder until the sound was overshadowed by the loud, grunted exclamation of Adam, "Oh FUCK!" His hands squeezed tightly against Alex's hips as he thrust himself up into her, deep and hard and excited, lifting her up on his erection and triggering another orgasm in her, one that stole her voice from her leaving Alex to squeal a silent, wordless scream of pleasure, brown eyes wide open and her mouth parted in a perfect O as all she could do was freeze up, body going rigid before breaking down into spasms of pleasure, helpless and brokenly collapsing down against Adam's limp form.

Risky Love

They did not move for what seemed like an eternity, just lay there, intermingled and intertwined, just finding pleasure in the next heated breath that they could pull into their lungs. Their limbs trembled and shone with the glossy afterglow of love making and when they did speak next it was not with their lips.

Chapter 10 -- The light of day

The rest of their time was spent sharing whispered, intimate words, the warmth of which cocooned around them in that blissfully warm haze that only lovers could know. Alex found out about Adam's four older brothers and how he, the youngest of them, would always be the butt of their jokes and cruel pranks and yet how the five of them were always inseparable.

Adam heard Alex talk about her awkward teenage years, about her last crush who had broken her heart and cheated on her and poisoned all possibility of love for her in the short term at least. The words were spoken with guarded hesitation, like peeling off the bandages off an old wound to check whether the hurt had healed or not.

They shared past secrets and joys, laughed with childish glee, naked in each other's arms and when the blanket of comfortable silence fell over them, they made love to each other one more time. This time a slower and more relaxed act. If their previous mating was an explosion of passion and conflict, raw, white hot pent up desire bursting forth, this was the sumptuous sampling of a feast.

This time she didn't hesitate, this time he didn't have to hold her against the door, this time she parted for him and wrapped herself around him and he sank himself deep into her and moved slowly, lazily, the fevered thrust of lust replaced by the hungry curiosity of passion. This time there was only silence accompanying them and they could each hear the heated music of each other's desire as they coiled together into each other, tasting, feasting, and reveling in the shared heat of their bodies.

This time Alex pressed her lips to Adam's and tasted the slight trembling of his mouth as he reached his orgasm and spilled it inside her. This time it was Adam who groaned the louder as he sank his hips down, pressing himself down to the very root inside of Alex and it was Adam who shuddered when Alex gently raked her nails down over his back, scratching long, instantly disappearing lines of crimson over his skin.

Neither one of them remembered falling asleep. Sleep just came over them seamlessly, effortlessly, they embraced it willingly, together. Alex was the first one to wake, her eyes fluttered as her gaze adjusted to the dim light of the store room, sunlight streamed through the high windows and Alex had to grope around for her phone to find more light.

She gasped as she unlocked her screen. 'You have 19 missed calls,' her soft groan woke Adam up. "What's going on?" he mumbled sleepily as he rolled over onto his back, his eyes frowned, valiantly trying to open against the stubborn pull of sleep.

Alex couldn't help but giggle before she leaned down and pressed a soft kiss to his forehead. "I have to go," she whispered softly against him and he nodded in response, kissing sleepily at air .

"Breakfast … coffee …" he mumbled groggily and Alex just giggled before running her fingers through his hair.

"Sure," she agreed sportingly to the barely worded proposal even as Adam drifted back to sleep.

Alex slid out of the store room with feline stealth, her stilettos carefully carried in one hand while with the other she nimbly tapped in her phone password and scrolled through the missed calls. Fifteen missed calls from dad, three from Cynthia and one from … Gabby?

Her heart skipped a beat and she stopped in her tracks in the middle of the now empty and messily cluttered nightclub. Somewhere an empty champagne bottle rolled on the floor with a grating rumble and for a moment that was the only sound going through Alex's head.

The sudden surge of panic subsided only to be replaced by the dull ache of guilt in her heart. How could she have done this? How could she have been this stupid, this selfish? Alex curled her hand into a fist and lightly bumped it against her forehead. "Stupid! Stupid! Stupid!" she muttered angrily before walking out of the club into the blindingly bright light of the day.

Taxis were easy enough to find and she slumped into the back of one. She could not deal with her father's concerns right now, she had no idea how she would react to him yelling at her about responsibility and being mature and a dozen other things he had been trying to drill into her head ever since she bought her first bra.

The driver dropped her off at her apartment. It was a studio apartment on the fifth floor of a building that had become the hallmark of hipsters, struggling artists and weed dealers, but it was her own and for now Alex desperately needed to clear her head and find some sort of breathing space.

"Hey." The sound startled Alex as she was just about to turn her key in her door. She turned around abruptly to find Gabby sitting on the flight of stairs that led up to the roof and faced her apartment door directly.

"Hey!" Alex gasped a reply, adding in a nervous giggle to the greeting, "What … uh … what are you doing here?" Alex bit on her lip at the obvious fidgetiness of her own voice.

Gabby smiled at her, it was a smile unlike Alex had ever seen on her, sad and knowing and mysterious all at the same time. A moment of silence, uncomfortable and awkward passed between them before Gabby stood up off the steps, brushed the dust from her legs and walked up to within an inch of Alex's face. Her words were spoken calmly, without any hint of emotion or glimmer of sentiment, "I know about you and Adam."

Chapter 11 -- Hallway confrontation

"You … know?" Alex repeated Gabby's words cautiously. Gabby nodded and sighed, the sound seeming strange coming from someone who by all rights should be furious and frenzied right now.

Alex bit her lip and leaned back against the door of her apartment with a defeated sigh. "How?" She whispered softly and Gabby just smiled at her.

"Alex, we have been friends since you were a sharpie junkie, do you REALLY think I wouldn't be able to tell who you have a crush on?"

Alex blinked at Gabby's words. "Crush?" A nervous smile crept over Alex's lips. "You think I have a crush on Adam?"

Gabby shrugged in reply, "Well … don't you? I mean all this … moody, grumpy sulkiness is obviously coming from somewhere and don't tell me it's a 'work thing'. I KNOW your work and clicking pictures of half-naked male models is NOT going to give anyone I know the blues."

Alex sighed again and squirmed uncomfortably against the door she still hadn't managed to open. "Look ... Gabby," she began only to be cut off by a raised hand.

"No ... YOU look. I have been your friend for the best part of two decades, I have been with you through thick and thin, through good and bad, for fuck's sake I stuck by you through that god-awful mullet phase of yours in high school, so don't you fucking tell me that there's nothing going on between you and Adam." The outburst was sudden and passionate and completely unlike Gabby, whom Alex had not seen this sincere and emotional since grade school.

"Gabby ..." Alex began gently before she bit down on her bottom lip. "It's ... not what you think."

Gabby smiled and shook her head gently. "Listen," she spoke, "Whatever it is, you have my blessings." Her hands squeezed against Alex's shoulders and gently kneaded them, "and please," she continued with a wry grin on her lips, "Don't EVER wear that skanky perfume ever again, my slut allergies are working up."

The sound of their laughter rang out in the mostly empty hallway and Alex felt a little bit of her guilt wash away in the sound of their shared laughter and before she knew it, her arms were around Gabby, holding her tight against herself, squeezing her in her grip as tight as she could. "I love you," Alex whispered softly, trying desperately not to let the trembling of her voice show through .

"I love you too," Gabby replied back, a smile in her voice and the sting of tears in her eyes.

The release was slow in coming and when it did, both of them had tears in their eyes. "Alright." Gabby spoke first, rubbing at her left eye with the back of her hand, "Quit being a little bitch."

Alex giggled again and wiped her hand against her eyes smudging her mascara over her cheeks. "You want to come in?" she asked Gabby in that same voice that she once used to ask her whether she wanted to play with her dolls.

Gabby smiled and shook her head at the request. "I better not darling, I have got a lot of stuff to do, besides …" she grinned as she leaned forward and bumped her forehead lightly against Alex's, "That would give your landlord all sorts of lesbian nightmares."

Alex laughed again, harder this time, genuine and guilt free. "Alright," Alex nodded with a smile, "I'll see you later?"

Gabby nodded at the question. "You'll see me later," and squeezed Alex's hand fondly.

Alex waited until Gabby had walked downstairs out of sight before turning to enter her own apartment and as soon as she closed the door of her room behind her the crushing weight of her betrayal came crashing down on her in a tidal wave of emotion that made her collapse on the floor.

She grabbed her knees against herself as she sobbed softly, her head resting on top of her knees as she trembled and sobbed, shaking her head side to side. She did not remember falling asleep on the carpeted floor of her room but that is where she woke up to the sound of a message beeping on her phone.

She wiped the sleep away from her eyes and looked out the window at the sky. It was already afternoon, she checked her phone, 2 pm, 'a day well wasted' she thought wryly to herself as she swiped her thumb across the screen to check the blinking message. It was a picture message from Gabby, she clicked on it and her heart froze at what it revealed.

Chapter 12 -- A picture IS worth a thousand words

Gabby fidgeted nervously with the hem of her dress as she walked the steps up to Adam's apartment. Her heels tapped lightly on the steps as she moved up them, slowly but surely. She had no idea what to say to him. This would be the first time she would be breaking up with a guy face to face, mostly it was via text or him discovering her on the arm of another, richer, more handsome man.

But Adam was different. She actually cared about him, however little, however tentatively; he deserved the proper courtesy of having an actual conversation before things ended with him, before she ended things with him.

Her soft, bottom lip clasped tightly between her teeth, she knocked lightly on his apartment door, which opened after the second knock, surprising her. "Hey," she managed through a nervous smile.

"Hey," Adam replied with a smile equally as nervous. "Come in," he said, "I was just coming to see you."

Gabby stepped into the apartment, slightly confused. "You … were?" she asked with a perplexed frown.

Adam sighed and nodded, one hand gently scratching at the back of his head. "Look … there's something we need to talk about," he began nervously.

"Wait," Gabby interrupted, "Before you say anything I just want to … to …" She frowned in the middle of her sentence, her nostrils flared at the smell of the familiar perfume. Where had she encountered that scent before? It wasn't hers, she was sure of it.

"Were you out last night?" she asked him cautiously, looking him up and down.

He was dressed casually but the clothes were far too designer to be worn indoors like this, and then it struck her like a punch to the gut. Alex had been out all night as well. She knew, she had waited outside her apartment for the better part of the night, had just left her at her apartment and the perfume.

God Almighty! The perfume was Alex's. Gabby looked up at Adam's face. He was saying something but she could not hear him, his lips were moving but all Gabby could hear was the high pitched whine of static in her ears and the sensation of a chill running through her, cooling her from the inside out.

She stepped forward towards Adam and he abruptly stopped talking. "Gabby?" he asked with a raised eyebrow. There was a look in her eyes that he had never seen before, nor for that matter had anyone who had ever known her seen that look, glazed and dark, like a shark in the deep.

She ignored his words and stepped another step closer, closing the distance between their bodies and leaned up, sealing his lips with her own.

"Gabby … stop," Adam whispered softly as he pressed his hands against her shoulders and gently pushed her back. "We can't do this." His words were soft and warm and a sharp contrast to the look in Gabby's eyes.

"I know …" she replied as she sank down onto her knees before him, her manicured slender fingers tinkering with his belt buckle.

"But one last time won't hurt, right?" she smiled seductively, that perfect predatory smirk that made men weak in the knees and hard in the loins. "One last time? Pretty please?" Her smile grew wider as she crawled forwards on all fours, exquisitely sensual and utterly hungry.

Adam took a step back, bumping against the door of his apartment. "Gabby … don't …" he groaned as she slipped her fingers past his open zipper and curled her fingers around the semi-flaccid girth within.

"Aww c'mon … Kitty wants her treat," she whispered with a warm sigh.

Her lips parted and closed over the head of Adam's cock, cheeks doubled inwards as she suckled hungrily with a wet vengeance and Adam closed his eyes, groaning as his head rolled back in pleasure.

CLICK!

The sound made his eyes snap open and he looked down at Gabby pointing the camera of her phone at herself, cock held between plump lips, taking a selfie. "What the hell …?" Adam growled in confusion as he pushed her off his cock angrily. "What do you think you're doing?"

Gabby grinned wickedly at the raised tone of his voice, her eyes locked with his even as her fingers tapped on the screen of her phone. "Just making us official," she licked at the corner of her mouth like a cat lapping blood off her fangs.

"There IS no us you crazy bitch," Adam snarled at her as he pulled his pants up and buttoned up. "You need to get the fuck out of here," he warned with an angry wag of his finger. "I mean it!" He stepped aside, opening the door for her. "RIGHT NOW!" his voice thundered in the emptiness of his apartment and Gabby just smiled in reply.

"Whatever you say lover," she purred even as she sashayed out the door with a triumphant grin on her lips.

Chapter 13 -- Rat fink

Alex sat on the floor of her room, motionless and utterly in shock, staring at the screen of her phone trying to make sense of what the picture was. She knew it was Gabby, she knew she had a penis between her lips, and she knew the penis belonged to Adam, but she still could not make sense of it at all.

She knew her best friend had just given her the go ahead to be with Adam, that Gabby had hugged her and told her that she was OK with it all. She also knew it was the same Gabby staring up with such venom in her eyes from the picture.

She knew all those things and yet she could not make heads or tails of it. 'I'm in shock' she thought to herself, 'this is what shock must feel like,' she repeated to herself as she chewed on the pad of her thumb nervously, a habit she thought she had abandoned in grade school, but some things never change apparently.

"Some things never change." She said the words out loud and somehow the sound of her own voice seemed to strengthen her, seemed to freeze away that protective layer of chill that her psyche had constructed against the realization of her friends betrayal.

She got up off the floor and walked over to the bedside mirror. Her hands clenched at the edges of the drawer as she just stared at herself in the mirror, anger and hurt and heartbreak roiling inside her like some lethal witches' brew, and in the middle of the tempest she came to a sudden revelation. Something that she ought to have realized years ago but as is the nature of revelations, it does not come until needed, and Alex sorely needed this revelation at this time.

She sighed and looked at herself in the mirror before sitting down and carefully wiping off the remains of her smudged mascara, her smeared lipstick and the remnants of whatever blush and foundation remained on her face. She dressed herself, out of her own closet, she wouldn't need fancy designer clothes for what she was about to do. She needed to be herself, black slacks and a simple loose top, her hair tied back and a pair of Converse sneakers on her feet that was all she needed.

She walked to the door and just as she reached for the handle it turned causing her to jump in surprise, even more so when the door opened to reveal Adam standing there.

"Wait!" Adam spoke first, pressing his hand against the door, anticipating the slam of it against his face. "Please … Alex … just listen to me."

Alex, for all her composure and mirror-staring and determination, seemed to find herself feeling utterly hateful towards him. Both her hands gripped against the edge of the door and tried to push it close. "Get out! Get out! GET OUT!"

Her loud shriek hid the trembling sound of a sob. She put her weight against the door and to her credit it even moved back an inch before Adam deftly slipped inside the door, allowing Alex to slam it shut behind him. "Look … I know you're angry and I can understand but … OW!" Adam yelped as a sneaker made contact with his head.

Alex had gotten her hands on her extensive collection of footwear, desperately searching through it for anything of weight and hardness to chuck at Adam's head. "You lying! … Cheating! … Rat Fink … BASTARD!" Each expletive punctuated by another sneaker or sandal or boot thrown at

Adam who managed to dodge most of them with graceful dexterity.

"Alex ... wait!" was all he managed before a particularly diabolical looking hard heeled designer shoe landed flat center on his face with a dull, sickening sound.

"Oh God!" Alex gasped in shock. She wasn't actually planning on hurting him like this, the carnage of shoe projectiles around her notwithstanding. "Oh no! ... shit!" she muttered as she rushed to Adam, who by this time was on his knees groaning and clutching at his face with both hands. "Adam! Adam are you ... MMPPHH!" and that was as far as Alex got before Adam pressed his lips to hers.

Both his hands cupped her face firmly but gently and insistently keeping their lips pressed together despite the weakening murmurs of protests spilling from her and which eventually melted away into a single, whimpering sound of hunger as her own hands came up to tangle and grip in his hair.

The kiss lasted for a good long minute, neither one of them moving, both of them joined together and just reveling in the existence of the other, and when it broke, it melted away with the delicacy of dissolving cream, the only words that were spoken between them were the heated murmurs of their breathing.

"I'm sorry," Adam spoke first, a trembling whisper of a sound that made Alex open her dark brown eyes up and look into his dark green gaze.

"You're an asshole," Alex murmured back and Adam laughed softly before tightening his arms around her.

"I know … but … if you want … I could be your asshole … wait …" Adam blinked at his own words, "that came out wrong … I mean…"

It was Alex's turn to laugh and she just shook her head, pressing her fingers to his lips delicately and smiling, "I know what you mean," she whispered back and leaned up pressing a kiss to his smiling mouth. "But I need you to mean it … I really do … that's the only way this works."

She looked into his eyes as she spoke, her gaze sincere and vulnerable and utterly honest.

"I mean it," Adam whispered and nodded, his arms wrapped around her waist and pulled her tightly against himself, lifting her onto the tips of her toes as he kissed her again, passionately this time, utterly and completely delving into the hunger of the kiss, his lips curving upwards as he felt Alex's doing the same.

Gabby could wait, Adam and Alex had a lot of making up to do.

THE END

Keep reading for a
Sneak Preview of
"CANDID LOVE",
Book 2
in the
Alexandra's
LOVE & ROMANCE
Series.

Sneak Preview of *CANDID LOVE*, Book 2

Chapter 1 -- Hawaiian hospitality

"Hawaiian Airlines welcomes you to Honolulu International Airport." The cheery voice of the flight attendant broke out over the public address system with an enthusiasm that Alex could barely stomach. She hated flying, always had, right from her first trip overseas with her family when she had spent the duration throwing up and suffering ear aches.

"The weather outside is a beautiful ninety degrees with the gorgeous Hawaiian sun shining down." Alex groaned softly and pressed her face into her hands, squeezing her palms against her eyes.

She really did not want to be this miserable, especially since she was just arriving in Hawaii for a one month, all expenses paid gig for one of the most respected modeling agencies in the world AND she was getting paid for it. Alex sighed and pulled up the complimentary night mask provided by the airline and peeked out at the interior of the plane as it started descending toward the runway.

Tourists in oversized, colorful Hawaiian shirts, families, couples, a few businessmen, and senior citizens huddled together in excited tour groups whispering eagerly while pointing at glossy tourism brochures. Alex smiled to herself despite the dull throbbing in her head and the barely restrained nausea. Life wasn't so bad after all.

Alex had taken this assignment despite the fact that it had been 'arranged' by her father. She had a fiercely independent streak in her, ironically inherited from her father and she hated being handed things.

There was a stubborn work ethic that touched all aspects of her life and caused her to work with Zen like dedication and focus. That was also part of why she had landed the gig.

The modeling agency she had been contracted to was known for its strict professional standards, for everything from the models they hired right down to the lighting crew and spot boys. All in all it had been her talent and professionalism that had gotten her the job. Her father had only made the introductions, but still it rankled her a great deal.

Her thoughts were interrupted when the tires of the plane made contact with the tarmac and the plane skidded and screeched, but only for a brief second before resuming its speedy path and finally taxiing to a stop. The mass of passengers started trickling out of the plane doors in a steady dribble and before she knew it Alex was standing in the Hawaiian sun.

She closed her eyes for a moment and breathed in deeply; the air was warm and bright and smelt of the sea. She smiled again as she felt her nausea dissipating in the warm tropical sun. She gathered her single carry on, her bottle of water and her hat and headed towards the baggage claims area, rubbing shoulders with enthusiastic Japanese tourists, tired parents herding hyperactive children and all of the rest of the people that had come to experience Hawaii.

She was greeted first at the gate with flowery garlands draped over her neck by beautiful grass skirt wearing females and then at the baggage carousel by the terrifying mass of humanity she had just shared a flying metal tube with. The next few minutes were a blur of loud raucous sounds, bumping trolleys and scuffed luggage. Apparently she wasn't the only one who had been eager to get off the plane.

The exit gate had another welcome for her, in the form of a gorgeous tanned, dark haired, brown-eyed island boy waiting with the most stunning smile she had seen. Her heart skipped a beat when she noticed the sign he was holding, a simple piece of cardboard paper with her name on it. She couldn't help the smile that spread over her lips as she made her way over to him.

"Miss Alexandra?" he asked, the most adorable accent in his voice. "Aloha!" he responded to the wordless smile on Alex's face, draping his arms around her in a warm, welcoming hug and hoisting another garland around Alex's neck.

"Lemme get dose for you," he offered gallantly and took Alex's bags from her.

Alex, who had forgotten her ordeal of flying and was just grinning ear to ear, mooning at the perfect example of Hawaiian hospitality, 'Nope' she thought to herself, 'Not a hard gig at all.'

Chapter 2-- Embarrassment and girlish delight

The inside of the car Alex stepped into was unlike anything she had seen before. Back in her hometown, cabs were a steady, uniformly decorated monolithic army of yellow and blue with one car completely indistinguishable from the next. What she was sitting inside, she could only describe as 'Inharmonious '.

There was a slew of feather boas and brightly colored drawing papers taped onto the walls in what she assumed was an attempt at decorating. Twin bobble headed luau girls wobbled their plastic necks on the dashboard of the car and the radio blasted Bob Marley unashamedly. If not for the glass divider between the driver and passenger, Alex would never have guessed that she was in a cab.

"So," she leaned forward and spoke loudly, trying to get herself heard over the sound of reggae music drifting out of the radio. "I'm Alex…" She offered tentatively and before she could react, he had turned around almost completely and stuck his hand through the window dividing the front and the back of the cab.

"Nico," he said happily, offering her his hand. "Pleased to meet you." Alex swallowed a small scream as Nico's turning around caused the cab to veer a little wildly on the road.

He drove as he decorated, unconventionally, unrestricted by norms or common sense and out of the lines. Alex's fingers clamped down onto the soft plush seat she was sitting on and she tried desperately not to sound like a complete dork.

"So...how long have you been driving a cab?" she asked trying to keep panic out of her voice as Nico barely managed to drive past an oncoming truck.

"Oh dis?" he looked down at the steering wheel he was so deftly managing to maneuver with just one hand. "Dis isn't my cab Alex," he grinned happily at the surprise on her face, "is my neighbors, just borrowing it to pick you up from the airport."

Another sharp swerve, another swallowed scream, Alex could feel her knuckles turning white. "So...uh...what's your neighbor doing today?" she asked trying to keep her mind off the escalating speedometer.

Nico shrugged at the question. "My gig down at the studio, jus' holding down t'ings you know?" He replied to her question as matter of fact, as if she had asked him what color the sky was.

He could sense the confusion in her look and glanced in the rear-view mirror to lock eyes with her. "Here we work different, yeah?" Alex couldn't help but smile at the utter simplicity and sincerity of his words.

She wondered how differently she would have to work now that she was here as well. "So you're not a cab driver, what are you?" She leaned forward, running her fingers through her hair trying to once again get herself heard over the sound of the radio.

Nico grinned into the rear-view mirror and Alex's heart thrilled at the twin little dimples that formed in his cheeks. "Whatever da lady wants." He shrugged with such a laid back, confident gesture that Alex couldn't help but match the smile he offered her.

"I'm a photographer, what can you help me with?" she teased him lightly, her own hazel eyes twinkling with playfulness.

Nico chuckled softly. "Oh a photographer? I don't trust photographers." He teased her right back. "All dey wan' do is get me out of my clothes and take loads of pictures for dem girly magazines."

Alex cupped her laughter in her hands and blushed lightly at the playful flirtation. "Shucks! You caught me out!" she replied, her voice still tingling with laughter.

Nico responded with another dazzling smile of his. "Yeah, I'm a sharp customer see?" following up the words with a playful wink.

Alex smiled softly and shook her head. It seemed like ages since she had had good, old fashioned flirty fun with a guy, since she had allowed herself to, ever since Adam. She sighed at the memory and leaned back into her seat, continuing to gaze out the window in silence.

The silence didn't last long though as only a few moments later Nico announced that they had arrived at the small villa resort the agency was renting out for staff over the course of the month. Alex smiled and couldn't help appreciate the muscles that bulged beneath tribal tattoos on Nico's arms as he helped her with her luggage.

"See you tonight?" Nico asked as Alex pushed the last of her bags into her room.

"What?" Alex blinked at his words; did he just ask her out on a date? Did she miss the asking out?

Nico laughed at the perplexed expression on her face. "Take it easy eh?" he grinned teasingly. "I only meant the welcome party tonight."

He grinned as he leaned forward, "And besides… you only want me for my body."

Alex blushed heatedly at the light teasing before cupping her face in one hand and nodding. "Yes Nico, you'll see me tonight," before closing the door behind her and squeaking into her palms with that sweet mixture of embarrassment and girlish delight. She peeked out from one of the windows as she heard his cab drive out towards the road and smiled softly to herself.

So far Hawaii was turning out to be an excellent choice.

Get your own copy now of "CANDID LOVE" to continue reading about Alexandra's adventures in love.

Dear Reader,

We hope you enjoyed this adventure-in-love story.

Make sure you don't miss out on new and exciting stories by our romance writer Triple D. Join our Preferred Customer list to stay in touch. You will get:

1. *Advance notice of new stories in the series*
2. *Special deals for preferred customers only*
3. *Flash news*

Go here to sign up now: <u>*www.denisedanielladarcy.com/newsletter*</u>

And everything is FREE!

Cheers,

Sally Carruthers, *Triple D's Helper*

Risky Love

Also by Denise Daniella Darcy

Samantha's
LOVE & ROMANCE Series

First Love – Book 1

Rebound Love Book 2

Cowboy Love – Book 3

Casual Love – Book 4

Denise Daniella Darcy

Also by Denise Daniella Darcy

Alexandra's

LOVE & ROMANCE Series

Risky Love – Book 1

Candid Love Book 2

Comic Con Love – Book 3

Special Love – Book 4

Risky Love

Hi Readers, Denise here. I am busy writing more stories about Alexandra's adventures in love so check my website www.DeniseDaniellaDarcy.com for the most up-to-date list. Happy reading! *DDD*

Denise Daniella Darcy

Other Titles By Durango Publishing Corp.®

YOUR 'Lose Weight FAST the Natural &
Healthy-Way DIET', a simple healthy
weight loss diet so YOU can live a
better, happier, more enjoyable life!

Horse Racing: Gambling to Win

Vegas Pro´s Best Racing Angles

Available at:

www.DurangoPublishing.com

&

Amazon

Recommended Reads

If you liked *RISKY LOVE*, check out these other great stories by popular authors.

Not Quite Dating (Not Quite series), Catherine Bybee

Tempting Her Best Friend (A What Happens in Vegas Novel), Gina Maxwell

Night Moves, Nora Roberts

Melt For Him (a Fighting Fire novel), Lauren Blakely

Midnight Betrayal, Melinda Leigh

About Denise Daniella Darcy

Denise Daniella Darcy, or Triple D as she is affectionately called by family, friends and fans, started life as a mortician's helper. Faced with the daily task of making the dead appear happy, she decided to switch careers and apply her talents to making the living happy instead. She achieves that through her Love & Romance novels. She writes from the heart, with a viewpoint that to grow you need to push your boundaries and you find happiness wherever it may appear and in any shape that it comes.

Triple D writes stimulating contemporary romances with passion, humor and a down to earth feel that resonates with her readers. She creates the 'I can't put the book down, just 1 more page before I turn out the lights' stories that keep you interested, engaged and involved.

Risky Love

Denise lives a vibrant and enthusiastic life on the west coast with a full house, including her children, cats and dogs, assorted critters, and her own personal hunk of a husband. The coffee is always on, the table always full of family and friends, and a spirited discussion is underway. And when evening rolls around, often enough a party is sent out to raid the wine cellar. Lively, fun and full of life.

Her Love and Romance novels include FIRST LOVE, REBOUND LOVE, COWBOY LOVE and CASUAL LOVE in the Samantha Series, as well as RISKY LOVE, CANDID LOVE, COMIC CON LOVE and SPECIAL LOVE in the Alexandra Series. In addition Triple D is busy writing a new series in the same romance genre featuring newcomer Charlotte.

To receive an email when Triple D releases a new novel, get on our FREE

newsletter   here:
www.denisedanielladarcy.com/newsletter.

And I know she'd love you to visit her at www.DeniseDaniellaDarcy.com.

Dear Reader,

One final note. Thank you so much for reading this story. I hope you really liked it.

As you probably know, many people look at the reviews on Amazon and Barnes & Noble before they decide to purchase a book.

If you liked the book, could you please take a minute to leave a 4 or 5 star review with your feedback?

You can do that right on the page where you found Risky Love.

60 seconds is all I am asking you for, and it would mean the world to me. Your friendly support will certainly help me in further research & writing.

Thank you so much, and here's to happy reading.

Denise Daniella Darcy

'Triple D' to my friends

PS. *Don't forget to get your* **FREE ALTERNATE ENDING** *here:*

http://www.denisedanielladarcy.com/riskylovealtending

Just my way of giving you something extra and thanking you for reading my books.

And if you have a friend who might like my novels, perhaps you could send her a link? As an indie writer I need friends to make any progress against the big guys.